The book for kids who
don't like to read books

Max Greenfield

Mike Newberg

I DON'T WANT TO READ THIS BOOK

WRITTEN BY
MAX GREENFIELD

ILLUSTRATED BY
MIKE LOWERY

putnam

G. P. Putnam's Sons

I
DON'T WANT
TO READ
THIS BOOK.

I KNOW
IT HAPPENS TO
BE THE TITLE OF
THIS BOOK,

BUT

LET ME MAKE MYSELF

VERY

CLEAR.

I

REALLY

DON'T WANT TO READ IT.

I MEAN, WHY WOULD I READ THIS BOOK?

I **ALREADY** KNOW WHAT'S GOING TO **HAPPEN.** I'M GOING TO OPEN UP THE FRONT COVER

ONLY TO FIND PAGES WITH,

LET ME GUESS...

SOMETIMES

A
LOT
OF WORDS.

(THIS IS NOT ONE OF THOSE PAGES.)

BUT THIS ONE IS

WORDS WORDS WORDS
WORDS WORDS
WORDS WORDS WORDS
WORDS
WORDS WORDS
WORDS WORDS WORDS WORDS
WORDS WORDS WORDS
WORDS
WORDS WORDS
WORDS WORDS
WORDS WORDS WORDS

LOOK, MOST WORDS ARE <u>FINE</u>

LIKE

AND

CAKE

YOUTUBE

BUT SOME WORDS ARE JUST PLAIN

RIDICULOUS.

TAKE THE WORD

DOUBT

FOR EXAMPLE.

WHAT IS A "B" DOING IN THERE ???

IF NO ONE CAN **HEAR** THE WHY DO WE HAVE TO **SEE** IT ???

I DOUBT WHOEVER PUT IT THERE WAS VERY SMART AT ALL.

OTHER WORDS ARE JUST TOO

BIG LIKE...

IN·FIN·I·

TES·I·MAL

IF YOU CAN BELIEVE IT, THIS WORD MEANS **SMALL** !!!

WORDS LIKE INFINITESIMAL ARE THE EXACT REASON

I DON'T WANT TO READ THIS BOOK.

AS IF WORDS WEREN'T
BAD ENOUGH,
I'M SURE THIS BOOK ALSO
HAS ITS FAIR SHARE OF

SENTENCES

WHICH ARE REALLY JUST

TOO MANY WORDS

ALL

SMUSHED

TOGETHER

WITH A **PERIOD** AT THE END.

SENTENCES ARE THE WORST!

I DON'T **EVER** WANT TO READ A BOOK THAT HAS SENTENCES IN IT...

PERIOD.

WHICH BRINGS ME TO

PARAGRAPHS.

I DO NOT UNDER ANY CIRCUMSTANCES WANT TO READ A BOOK WITH A SINGLE PARAGRAPH IN IT.

Did you know that a paragraph can be more than half a page long? I have seen some that take up an ENTIRE page!

I MEAN, WHAT ARE THESE PARAGRAPHS TRYING TO PROVE?

JUST LOOKING AT A PARAGRAPH EXHAUSTS ME.

ALL OF THOSE WORDS!

AS IF ANYONE ON EARTH

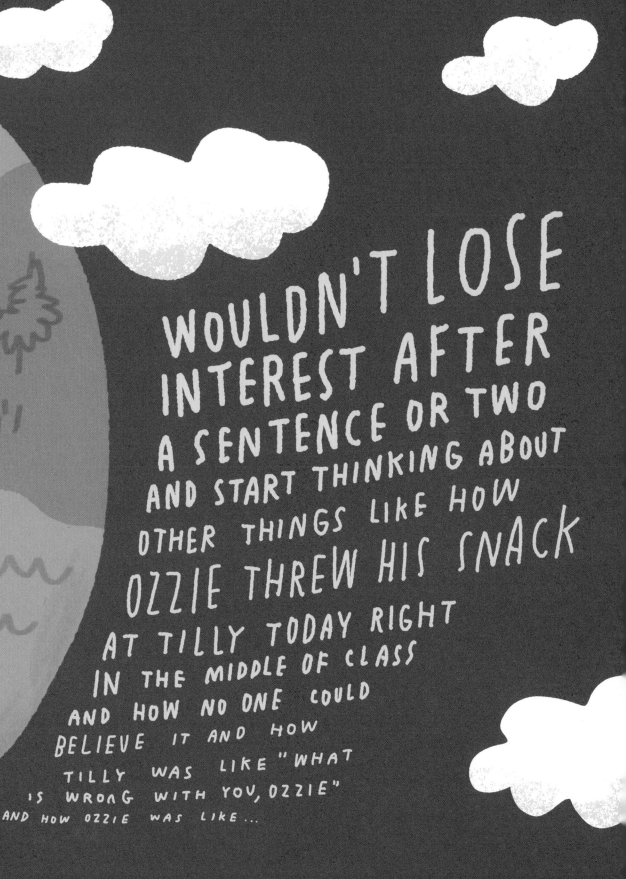

WOULDN'T LOSE
INTEREST AFTER
A SENTENCE OR TWO
AND START THINKING ABOUT
OTHER THINGS LIKE HOW
OZZIE THREW HIS SNACK
AT TILLY TODAY RIGHT
IN THE MIDDLE OF CLASS
AND HOW NO ONE COULD
BELIEVE IT AND HOW
TILLY WAS LIKE "WHAT
IS WRONG WITH YOU, OZZIE"
AND HOW OZZIE WAS LIKE...

WAIT A MINUTE.

WHERE WAS I AGAIN?

PARAGRAPHS.

I don't want to read any book that has a paragraph in it. Paragraphs belong in chapter books, and chapter books are for people with nothing better to do.

CHAPTER 2

I Still Don't Want to Read This Book

ALL THE THINGS I COULD BE DOING THAT ARE MORE IMPORTANT THAN READING THIS BOOK:

1 EATING CAKE

2 EATING CAKE WHILE WATCHING YOUTUBE

3 WATCHING YOUTUBE AND <u>NOT</u> EATING CAKE

 BUT TRUTH BE TOLD, I PREFER TO BE EATING CAKE.

MY BRAIN HURTS
AND MY EYES FEEL TIRED.
READING THIS BOOK HAS BEEN A TRULY
MISERABLE
EXPERIENCE FOR ME.

I CAN'T BELIEVE I'M ALMOST DONE WITH THIS BOOK.

I DID NOT WANT TO READ IT!

AFTER I'M DONE, I'M GOING TO NEED SOME SPACE.

UGH,
I REALLY DON'T WANT TO READ THE LAST PAGE.
I ALREADY KNOW WHAT IT'S GOING TO SAY.
IT'S HOW ALL BOOKS END.
AS IF ANYTHING COULD BE MORE PREDICTABLE.

LET'S JUST
GET IT OVER
WITH, I GUESS...

I CAN'T BELIEVE
I JUST READ THIS BOOK.

THE CHANCES OF IT EVER HAPPENING AGAIN ARE

INFINITESIMAL.

SOME

SPACE

To my daughter, Lilly
(the brains of the operation).
—M.G.

Dedicated to Allister.
You are one of my favorite
things on this planet.
—M.L.

G. P. Putnam's Sons
An imprint of Penguin Random House LLC, New York

First published in the United States of America by G. P. Putnam's Sons,
an imprint of Penguin Random House LLC, 2021
Text copyright © 2021 by Max Greenfield
Illustrations copyright © 2021 by Mike Lowery

G. P. Putnam's Sons is a registered trademark of Penguin Random House LLC.

Visit us online at penguinrandomhouse.com

Library of Congress Cataloging-in-Publication Data is available.

Manufactured in China by RR Donnelley Asia Printing Solutions Ltd.

ISBN 9780593326060

1 3 5 7 9 10 8 6 4 2

Design by Eileen Savage.
Text set in Pitch Or Honey Sans.
The art in this book was done first with pencils and then with digital media.